WITHDRAWN
FROM THE RECORDS OF
MID-CO
USBOR
D0571886

JE
Punter, Russell.
The scaredy cat

MID-CONTINENT PUBLIC LIBRARY
Parkville Branch
8815 N.W. 45 Highway
Parkville, MO 64152
PV

The SCAREDY Cat

Russell Punter

Illustrated by Gustavo Mazali

Reading Consultant: Alison Kelly
Roehampton University

There was once a cat who lived in a big town.

His name was Stanley.

But everyone called him Scaredy Cat...

...because he was scared of everything.

He was scared of planes...

MID-CONTINENT PUBLIC LIBRARY
Parkville Branch
8815 N.W. 45 Highway
Parkville, MO 64152
PV

...and trains.

He was scared of boys...

...and noise.

He was scared of heights...

...and kites.

He was scared of frogs...

...and dogs.

Stanley was the biggest scaredy cat in town.

One night, Stanley went for a walk with his friends, Tabby and Snowy.

Something small and furry ran past. A mouse!

"Let's chase it," said Tabby.
"Let's not," cried Stanley.

The mouse ran into a house.

"It looks like no one is home," said Snowy.

"Here's a cat flap," said Tabby. "Let's go in."

"What if the house is haunted?" said Stanley. He shivered.

But he followed his friends inside.

"Now where's that mouse?" said Tabby.

Suddenly, the mouse ran across the hall and down to the cellar.

"This way!" said Snowy.

Snowy and Tabby raced downstairs.

"It's too dark down there," said Stanley. "I'll stay here."

Now Stanley was all alone, he felt *really* scared.

"M...m...maybe I should have gone with them after all," he thought.

Just then, Stanley felt a bump. Something was in the lounge.

"W...w...what was that?" he wondered.

It went "Bang..."

"Bang!"

"Bang!"

"Come quickly, Snowy!" called Stanley. "There's a giant in the lounge."

Snowy raced up the stairs. "A giant?" he cried. "Are you sure?"

Snowy crept into the lounge.

"It's just a window banging," Snowy said.

"Well, it *could* have been a giant," said Stanley.

"You're such a scaredy cat," said Snowy. "I've got a mouse to catch."

Snowy ran back downstairs.

Just then, Stanley heard a noise. Something was in the bathroom.

"W...w...what was that?" he wondered.

It went "Woo..."

"Wooo!"

"Woooo!"

"Come quickly, Tabby!" called Stanley. "There's a ghost in the bathroom."

Tabby raced upstairs. "A ghost?" he cried. "Are you sure?"

Tabby crept into the bathroom.

"It's only the wind,"
Tabby said.

"Well, it *might* have been a
ghost," said Stanley.

"You're such a scaredy cat," said Tabby. "I've got a mouse to catch."

Tabby ran back downstairs.

Just then, Stanley saw a lump behind the curtains.

"W...w...what's that?" he wondered.

It went "Grunt..."

"Grunt!"

"Grunt!"

"Come quickly, Snowy!" yelled Stanley. "There's a monster in the lounge."

"I don't believe you," called out Snowy.

The monster came closer.

"Come quickly, Tabby!" yelled Stanley. "There really is a monster in the lounge."

"I don't believe you,"
called out Tabby.

The monster came
closer still.

It came closer... and
closer... and closer.

Now it was right
on top of Stanley.

Stanley tried to run. But he was frozen to the spot with fear.

The monster tripped over Stanley.

It got tangled in the curtain...

spun around and
around...

and fell, with a
thud! on the floor.

Snowy and Tabby
came upstairs.

The lady who lived in the house came home.

A head came through the curtains.

But it wasn't a monster.

The lady stroked Stanley. "Looks like you just caught a burglar, kitty-cat."

For the first time in his life, Stanley felt brave.

The lady gave Stanley a special reward for catching the burglar.

From then on, Stanley wasn't afraid of anything.

And no one called him a scaredy cat ever again.

Series editor:
Lesley Sims

First published in 2008 by Usborne Publishing Ltd., Usborne House, 83-85 Saffron Hill, London EC1N 8RT, England. www.usborne.com
Copyright © 2008 Usborne Publishing Ltd.

All rights reserved. No part of this publication may be reproduced, stored in a retrieval system or transmitted in any form or by any means, electronic, mechanical, photocopying, recording or otherwise, without the prior permission of the publisher. The name Usborne and the devices are Trade Marks of Usborne Publishing Ltd.
Printed in China. UE. First published in America in 2009.

48

USBORNE FIRST READING
Level Four

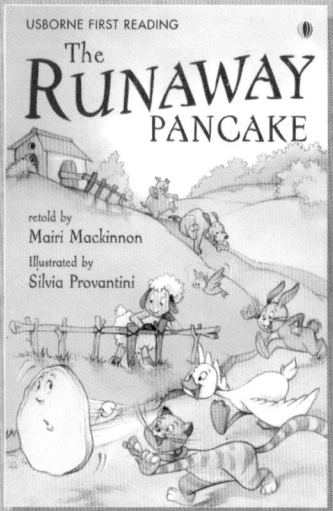

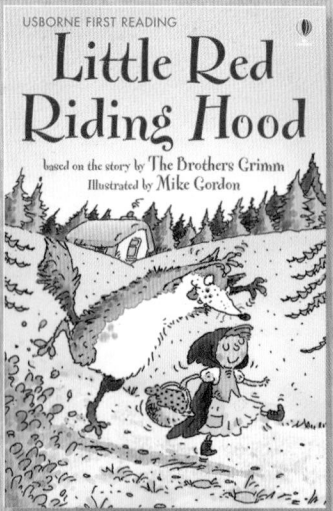